"Hands that don't want to work make you poor.
But hands that work hard bring wealth to you."
(Proverbs 10:4)

"Let's all do the hop, Oh Baby, let's all do the hop."
Jimmy and Jerry sang as they entered the Veggie-HOP café. Junior and
Laura were busy working to raise money for the VeggieTown Hospital.

Cool Hand Cuke

By Cindy Kenney
Illustrated by Michael Moore

BIG IDEA
BOOKS®

ZONDERVAN.com/
AUTHORTRACKER
follow your favorite authors

BIG IDEA BOOKS®

www.bigidea.com

ZONDERkidz™
.com

Cool Hand Cuke
Copyright © 2005 by Big Idea, Inc.
Illustrations © 2005 by Big Idea, Inc.

Requests for information should be addressed to:
Grand Rapids, Michigan 49530

Library of Congress Cataloging-in-Publication Data

Kenney, Cindy, 1959-
  Cool Hand Cuke / by Cindy Kenney.
      p. cm. -- (VeggieTown values ; bk. 5)
      "VeggieTown Adventures."
   Summary: After quitting his summer job at the Veggie-Hop Cafe, Junior Asparagus
learns about giving when a book transports him to a chicken farm, where he meets
two characters who do more than raise funds for their local hospital.
   ISBN-13: 978-0-310-70738-7 (softcover)
   ISBN-10: 0-310-70738-2 (softcover)
 [1. Charity--Fiction. 2. Generosity--Fiction. 3. Conduct of life--Fiction. 4.
Vegetables--Fiction.] I. Title. II. Series.
   PZ7.K3933Coo 2006
   [Fic]--dc22
                                                              2005025153

Written by: Cindy Kenney
Illustrated by: Michael Moore
Editor: Amy Devries
Art direction & design: Karen Poth

Printed in Hong Kong

08 09 10 11 12 • 12 11 10 9 8 7 6 5 4 3

"Junior!" shouted Laura. "Customers!"

Junior rolled his eyes. He dragged himself away from his peanut-butter milk shake and seated Jimmy and Jerry.

Laura took an order at another table.

"Do you have zee French fries?" asked Jean Claude.

"Or zee French toast?" asked Phillipe.

"No," Laura explained. "Everything we serve at the House of Peanut Butter has peanut butter in it."

"Order up!" called the cook.
Laura spotted Junior sitting with Jimmy and Jerry. "Junior! Please get that order!"
"We're not raising much money," Junior moaned.
"C'mon Junior, please!" Laura begged. "It will be worth it, you'll see."

"It's not worth it. I'm wasting my whole summer vacation and I won't have a thing to show for it," Junior grumbled as he jumped out of the booth.

He didn't see Laura, who was carrying a tray full of peanut-butter fritters.

CRASH!

"That's it. I quit," Junior said and stomped out the door.

That evening Junior wandered into the Treasure Trove Bookstore.
"What's got your feathers all ruffled, lad?" Mr. O'Malley asked.
"I don't want to work during summer vacation if I don't get to keep the money" Junior said.

"Looking to get rich, are ya?" the Irish potato said with a wink.
Wham! A big book plopped down in front of Junior.
"A vacation book?" Junior asked.
"Better than that. It's a trip to a farm where you'll find real wealth."
Junior read the title, "Cool Hand Cuke."

As he opened the book, the words "Once Upon A Time" began to swirl around and . . .

WHOOOOOOOOOOOOSH!

Junior found himself racing **down**

down

down

right into the middle of a farm.

"Ah! The new farmhand," a tomato said.

"I'm Hot Hand Tomato," he said. "This is my partner, Cool Hand Cuke."

He shoved a basket at Junior and said, "We've got lots of work to do before sundown. You can help us finish up in the barn."

"This is supposed to be my vacation," whined Junior.

In the barn they were greeted by a grape with mirrored sunglasses.
"If you fill your baskets before sundown, you get a prize from the box,"
barked the grape. "If you feed the chickens by ten, you get a prize from the
box. Sweep the barn by noon, and you get a prize from the box."

Junior glanced at the prize box. It contained lots of stuff like a yo-yo, tennis shoes, and a sombrero, but not riches.

"Finishin' up over here, boss," said Cool Hand Cuke. He showed him a full basket of eggs.

"Pick your prize out of the box, Cuke," said the boss.

Cool Hand Cuke eyed a big, colorful sombrero. "Oooh, I'm going to wear this into town! Junior, Hot Hand, would you come too?"

"Thanks!" Junior said. "That's better than collecting a bunch of eggs and sweeping a dirty old barn!"

When they got to town, Cool Hand Cuke and the tomato hung a sign over a booth. It read: Eggs for Sale.

"Oh, I get it," Junior said. "This is how we get rich! We sell the eggs so we can go on vacation. Good idea."

The eggs sold like crazy. Their job complete, Junior, Cool Hand Cuke, and Hot Hand Tomato headed toward the city hospital.

Doctors, nurses, and patients filled the room. "What's going on?" asked Junior.

"Time for a square dance!" Cool Hand shouted.

"There are only three of us," Hot Hand whispered. "We can't make a square. How about a triangle?"

"Excellent idea!" agreed Cool Hand. Two gourds called out commands as Cuke, Hot Hand, and Junior began to do-si-do.

"Isosceles!"

"Right angle!"

"Look how happy we're making the patients," whispered Hot Hand.

When the music stopped, Hot Hand called for a break. "I'll make the tamales!"

"I'll get the drinks," Cuke offered. He headed toward the watercooler. "Sure wish we had something special to give them besides tamales."

"Do you have any peanut butter?" Junior asked.
Junior whipped up some peanut-butter shakes and served the patients.
Cool Hand Cuke got ready for his juggling act.

"Everybody loves this," the tomato whispered.
"Juggle thirty eggs today, Cuke!" yelled a pea.
"Forty!" chimed in another.
"Fifty!" called the gourds.
"Nobody can juggle fifty eggs!" shouted a nurse.

"I can!" boasted the cucumber. "That's why they call me Cool Hand Cuke."
Everyone cheered as Cool Hand Cuke began to juggle. Ten . . . twenty . . .
thirty . . . forty . . . and then fifty eggs!

After the party, Cuke removed his sombrero. It was filled with the money from the eggs they'd sold.

Junior's eyes popped open. "We're rich!"

"This money is for the hospital," said Cuke.
"But weren't we working to get rich?"
"What we have here is a failure to appreciate," said the tomato.
"What does that mean?" asked Junior.

"Junior, we are rich. Look at that little carrot over there. See the smile on her face? And the pea over there? See how happy he is to have a new wheel-chair? We are rich in friendship and love," Cuke said.

Hot Hand showed Junior a card the patients had made. It said two simple words: THANK YOU!

"God says, 'Hands that don't want to work make you poor. But hands that work hard bring wealth to you,'" the tomato explained.

"I've got a whole summer ahead of me! Just think what I can do for others!" Junior smiled.

Just then two words floated out of the speakers: **THE END**.
Junior was swept up into the spinning letters.

After Junior landed back in the bookstore he rushed over to the café. "I'm really sorry," Junior told Laura. "I'll help you raise money for the VeggieTown Hospital. Maybe we could even provide entertainment."

"Really?" Laura asked.

"You bet! After all, hands that don't want to work make you poor. But hands that work hard bring wealth to you."

Junior began clearing the tables. Laura smiled at her friend. "What kind of entertainment did you have in mind?"

"Do you know how to juggle eggs?"